6|9|11

6(9

Vampire School
Stage Fright

For Theo and Tara
P.B.

For my Dad'

First published in Great Britain in 2011
by Boxer Books Limited.

www.boxerbooks.com

Based on an original idea by Chris Harrison
Text copyright © 2011 Peter Bently
Illustrations copyright © 2011 Chris Harrison

The illustrations were prepared using biro and watercolour paints
The text is set in Blackmoor Plain and Adobe Caslon

ISBN 978-1-907967-01-6

1 3 5 7 9 10 8 6 4 2

Printed in Great Britain

All of our papers are sourced from managed forests and renewable resources.

Vampire School

Stage Fright

Written by Peter Bently

Illustrated by Chris Harrison

Boxer Books

Contents

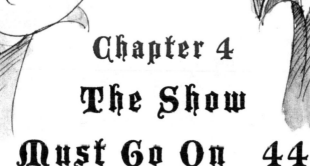

Chapter 1
Ghoul Show

The school clock was striking nine when a small bat zoomed up to the main entrance of St. Orlok's Primary School. The bat hovered in front of the doors for a moment, then with a POP! it turned into a boy. It was Lee Price, and he was late for school. Vampire school.

Lee dashed through the doors
– and almost crashed right
into Mr E. Gore, the school
caretaker.

"Hey! Votch vere you're
going!" grumbled Mr Gore.

"Sorry!" called Lee, speeding
down the corridor with his
black cape flapping behind him.
"Late again, huh?" yelled
Mr Gore.
He shook his fist so hard
that little flakes of rotten
skin flew off it like green
dandruff. "Pesky vampire kids!
So unreliable! Ve zombies are
alvays dead on time!"
Lee reached his classroom and

burst in just as his teacher, Miss Gargoyle, was taking the register. All the other young vampires turned to stare at him.

"Sorry I'm late, Miss!" he gasped breathlessly, plonking himself down at a table next to his friends Billy Pratt and Bella Williams.

"Really, Lee," sighed Miss

Gargoyle. She peered at the clock. "I nearly marked you absent. Tonight of all nights!"

"Sorry, Miss. I forgot my costume and had to go back home for it."

"Good grief!" panicked Miss Gargoyle. "Has anyone else forgotten their phantomime costume?"

Snow Fright
and the
Seven Dwarfs

"No, Miss Gargoyle!"
chorused the class.
"Thank goodness for that,"
said Miss Gargoyle with relief.
"There's enough to think about
as it is!"
Later that night Miss Gargoyle's
class was performing Snow
Fright and the Seven Dwarfs

in the school hall. Lee had the part of Gnashful, the dwarf who was always cross. "Mith Gargoyle! Mith Gargoyle!" piped up Lucy West, who was going to be the Wicked Queen. "My cothtume is bound to be the betht. Shall

I show it to the clath?"
"Typical West the Pest,"
whispered Bella. "Any excuse
to show off!" Bella was playing
Princess Snow Fright.
"I know,"
agreed Lee.

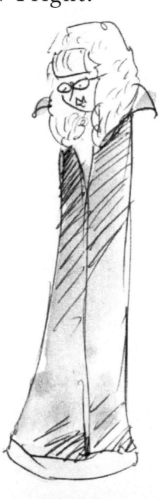

"At least she's stopped
boasting about how many
fangs she's lost."

"Yeah," said Billy, who was
playing the hunter who took
Snow Fright into the forest.

"And about how the Fang
Fairy gives her two pounds for
each fang."
Lucy scowled at them and
stuck her tongue out.
"We'll see all the costumes
after break, when we have our

dress rehearsal," said Miss Gargoyle firmly. "Until then it's lessons as usual."

"Aw, Miss!" groaned the class.

"Quiet please, everyone!" said Miss Gargoyle. "Today we are going to practise the Three S's. Does anyone know what that stands for?"

"What about Scaring, Staring and Startling?" suggested Bella.

"Or Shrieking, Screaming and Screeching?" said Big Herb, secretly popping three sweets into his mouth when he thought Miss Gargoyle wasn't looking.

"More like Scoffing, Slurping and Stuffing Your Face," chuckled Lee. Nobody had been surprised when Miss Gargoyle had chosen Herb to play Chompy, the greediest of the Seven Dwarfs.

"Good guesses," said Miss Gargoyle, neatly swiping Big Herb's hidden stash of sweets. "But to begin with let's all turn into bats."

Everyone said the words that Miss Gargoyle had taught them:

'I'm a bat, a bat is me
A bat is all I want to be.'

And with a volley of soft POPs they all became bats, fluttering merrily round the classroom.

Big Herb managed it on his
second go. First time around
his mouth was so full of sweets
that he said mat instead of
bat and turned into a flying
carpet.

"Now listen and watch carefully," squeaked Miss Gargoyle, who was now a little brown bat. "The first two S's are Swooping and Swerving."

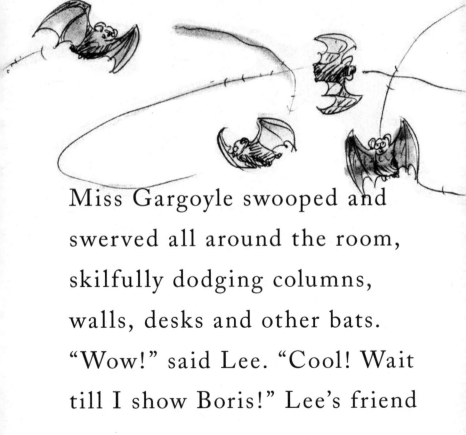

Miss Gargoyle swooped and swerved all around the room, skilfully dodging columns, walls, desks and other bats. "Wow!" said Lee. "Cool! Wait till I show Boris!" Lee's friend

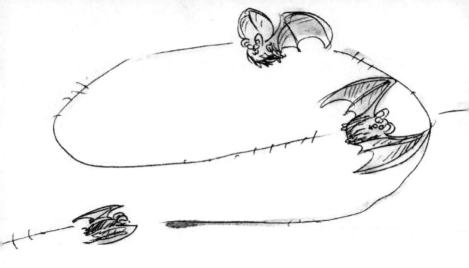

Boris was a real bat who lived
in the school clock tower.
Miss Gargoyle hovered in
mid-air to get her breath back.
"The third S," she went on, "is
Skulking. This is particularly
handy when you need to
turn into a bat – or back
into a vampire – without any
Fangless folk seeing you.

When you need
a place to skulk,
my tip is to
remember the
Three C's: Columns, Curtains
and Corners."
"What sort of corners?" said Lee.
"Three-D ones are best," said

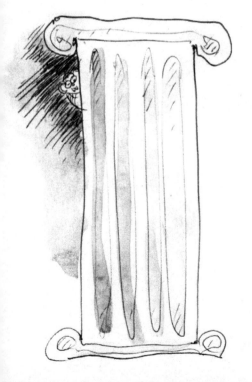

Miss Gargoyle.

"What?" asked Billy. "As in a 3-D movie?"

"No," said Miss Gargoyle. "As in Dark, Damp and Dingy. Right class, now you all have a go." They practised the Three S's until the bell rang for break.

"Well done, everybody," said Miss Gargoyle. "That's lessons finished for today. See you after break in the school hall for the dress rehearsal." She glanced over at Lee. "And don't forget your costumes!"

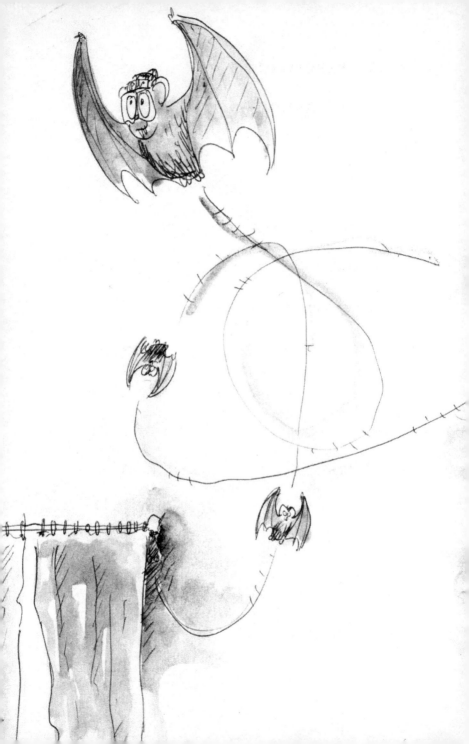

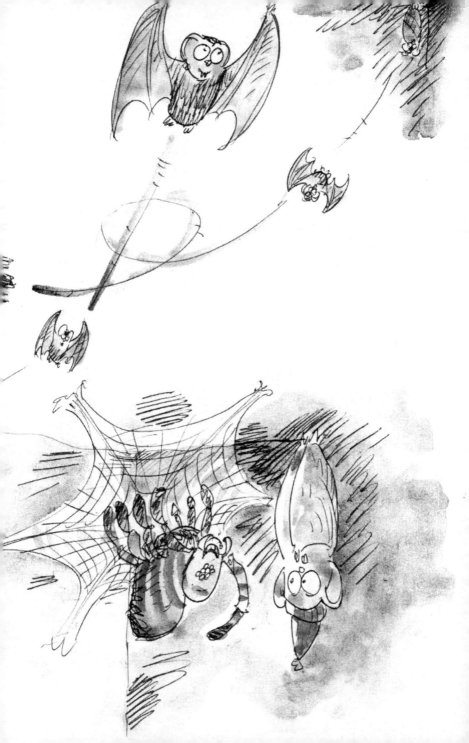

Chapter 2
First Night Nerves

At break Lee, Bella and Billy sat together. Lee tucked into a packet of Drac's Snacks, but Billy and Bella ate hardly anything at all.

"I – I can't eat," quivered Billy. "I'm so nervous about this stupid phantomime. I dunno why I said I'd be in it. I hate acting!"

"You'll be fine," said Lee.

"The hunter hasn't got much to say, not like—"

"ATCHOO!"

Bella sneezed so loudly that Lee dropped his snack and Billy almost jumped out of his seat.

"Yikes, Bella!" said Lee.

"That was loud enough to wake up a zombie!"

"Sorry," said Bella. "I've got a bit of a cold. I don't think I should have done so much skulking during the last lesson."

"Well, you did manage to find the darkest and dampest corner," said Billy. "It took us ages to spot you."

"My throat feels funny too," said Bella.

"You're probably just nervous," said Lee. "After all,

you have got the biggest part."

"And you've got to sing those songs all on your own," Billy chipped in. Miss Gargoyle had asked Bella to play Snow Fright because she had the best voice in the class.

"Yeah," said Lee. "In front of the whole school."

"And lots of parents and friends," said Billy.

"Oh thanks, guys!" groaned Bella. "You've really cheered me up!"

Lee hastily changed the subject.

"Miss Gargoyle said there's going to be a special mystery guest," he said. "I wonder who it is?"

"No idea," said Billy. "Didn't she say the Mayor is coming? Maybe it's him."

"Oh, durrr!" snorted Bella.

"The whole point of a mystery guest is that you don't know who it is, silly."

"All right," said Billy. "Keep your cape on!"

"It's no good," said Bella. "I just can't eat. Does anyone want my snack?"

Big Herb was at the next table. Hearing the offer of free food he whizzed round like a tornado.

"I'll have it!" he said through a huge mouthful of black pudding sandwich, some of which sprayed out onto his jumper. Then he looked at Bella's tub of beetroot salad and shook his head. "Yurggh! Actually, no thanks Bella. I forgot you're a vegetarian."

Chapter 3
Snow Fright in a Flap

After break Lee, Bella and Billy went straight to the hall and changed into their phantomime costumes.

"OK, Seven Dwarfs," said Miss Gargoyle. "Let's run

through the Work Song one last time."

Lee and the six other vampire dwarfs all marched across the stage in a line. They were Gappy, Snappy, Flappy, Creepy, Chompy, Gnashful and Shock.

As they marched they sang—

"POP-POP! POP-POP!
We'll work until we stop!
We're a scary sight,
But we won't bite!
POP-POP! POP-POP!"

On the final POP! they
all changed into bats and
fluttered off into the wings.

"POP!" *"POP!"*

"POP!"

"POP!"

"Excellent!" said Miss
Gargoyle. "Now let's hear
Snow Fright's song."

Bella stood up and opened
her mouth.

"Some day my Count will –
URK!"

She coughed and started again.

"Some day – URK!" Bella spluttered to a halt. "I can't do it!" she croaked faintly. "I've lost my voice!"

"Oh dear!" said Miss Gargoyle anxiously. "What are we going to do? We can't do Snow Fright and the Seven Dwarfs without Snow Fright!"

"Perhaps someone else could be Snow Fright?" suggested Lee.

Lucy West stepped forward.

"I'll do it, Mith Gargoyle!" she said. "I've learnt all the wordth. And I can thing much better than Bella any day," she bragged.

Bella glared at Lucy, but Miss Gargoyle said, "Sorry, Lucy. If you play Snow Fright we'll just need someone else to play the Wicked Queen. We'll be back where we started."

"And no one could be a better Wicked Queen than you, Lucy," said Lee innocently. "You're perfect for the part!"

He winked at Bella as Lucy stomped off with her nose in the air.

"What we need," said Miss Gargoyle, "is someone who can sing but hasn't got much to do."

"But it's too late for anyone else to learn the words!" rasped Bella. "Oh, the phantomime is going to be ruined and all because of me. I'm so sorry!"

"Hang on," said Lee. "I've got an idea..."

Chapter 4
The Show Must Go On

The show began at three o'clock. At a quarter to three, Lee's mum and dad arrived backstage with his friend Ollie Talbot, who went to Chaney Street First School for young werewolves.

"Hi Ollie," said Lee, who was now dressed as a vampire

dwarf, with a short green cape, pointy red hat and a false ginger beard.

"Hi Lee," said Ollie. "Cool costume! You should wear that to school every day."

"Ha-ha, very funny," said Lee. "This beard itches like anything! I hate having hair all over my face."

"Oh, you get used to it," grinned Ollie.

"Good luck, Lee," said Dad cheerfully. "Seeing you on stage takes me back to my days with the Bat City Strollers.

Did I ever play you our recording of Fang-A-Lang? It got to number 98 in 1979."

"Yes Dad," sighed Lee. "Only about a million times."

"Bother!" came Billy's voice behind them. They turned to see Billy, dressed as the hunter, struggling to untangle his bow from the folds of Snow Fright's cape.

"Don't pull so hard," said Bella. "You'll tear it!"

Billy finally yanked the bow free.

"It's bad enough trying to remember my lines without having to carry this stupid bow," he moaned. "It just gets in the way!"

"Just relax," said Lee. "You'll be fine. You're only on in the first bit."

Lee's mum looked at her watch.

"Five to three!" she said. "We'd better get back to our seats. The hall's almost full. All the parents have come, and lots of friends, as well as a party of werewolves from Ollie's school. I've spotted several mummies too, and there's even a row of zombies right next to us. But I think they've fallen asleep."

"No they haven't," said Ollie. "They always look like that."

Mum blew Lee a kiss.

"Good luck, darling. And try not to look so cross. I'm sure it'll all be fine!"

"I'm Gnashful," said Lee. "I'm meant to look cross!"

"Right," said Miss Gargoyle
after Mr and Mrs Price and
Ollie had taken their seats.
"It's three o'clock. Let's go for it!"

She strode out in front of
the audience. "Good evening

everyone! The children have
all worked really hard for
tonight's show and we hope
you enjoy it. I have great
pleasure in presenting Snow

Fright and the Seven Dwarfs!"

She returned backstage and smiled at the children.

"Ready, Wicked Queen?"

"Yeth Mith Gargoyle," simpered Lucy West. Lee, Bella and Billy had to admit that she did look rather splendid in her Wicked Queen costume.

As the applause died down the Wicked Queen stepped through a cardboard doorway onto the stage. She stood in front of her magic mirror and declared:

*"Mirror, mirror
on the wall,
Who is the fairetht
of them all?"*

The phantomime had
begun.

Chapter 5
A Screaming Success

There was one dodgy
moment near the start of the
phantomime. Billy was so
nervous that he accidentally

knocked the Wicked Queen's pointy hat off with his bow. The audience found it very funny, especially when Lucy hissed, "You thtupid idiot! You've methed up my hair!"

But things went smoothly after that. There were no more mishaps and no one forgot their lines. Even Bella appeared to have found her voice again when she came on as Princess Snow Fright. She was a little husky and faint when she spoke, but she sang as sweetly as anything:

"One day my Count will come,
With sharp fangs he's not so dumb.
To his creepy castle I'll ride
By my spooky sweetheart's side."

"That was lovely," whispered Lee's mum.

"Yes," agreed Mr Price. "But I thought all the dwarfs were in this bit? There are only six of them."

"You're right," said Mrs Price. "Where's Lee?"

It was curious. Gappy, Snappy, Flappy, Creepy, Chompy and Shock were all sitting in their cottage around the fire – but Gnashful was nowhere to be seen.

Lee reappeared in the next scene, when the dwarfs flew home as bats and changed back into vampires – only to find Snow Fright in a faint from the Wicked Queen's poisoned apple.

But after Count Alarming had saved Snow Fright, Lee vanished again just before she sang her song for the last time.

"Look!" whispered Ollie to Lee's mum. "He's behind that tree."

"Which one?" whispered Mrs Price.

"The blue one," said Ollie. "Next to Snow Fright."

Ollie was right. After Bella's song Mrs Price spotted Lee slipping out from behind the tree to join the other dwarfs. He was just in time to watch the Wicked Queen scream in fury – Lucy was very good at screaming – and disappear in a puff of smoke.

"And that," chorused the dwarfs, "was the end of the Wicked Queen. And Snow Fright and Count Alarming lived snappily ever after."

The children all took a bow amid cheers and clapping. Ollie and the other werewolves bayed and howled,

and the mummies flapped
and waved their bandages.
The phantomime had been a
terrific success.

Mr and Mrs Price and Ollie
left their seats to go backstage
and congratulate Lee.

"Excuse us," said Mr Price,
as they pushed along the row
of zombies. The zombies were

the only ones not applauding
wildly.

They sat in total silence,
staring blankly at the stage. As
Ollie went past, one of them
turned to his wife.

"Mildred, my dear," muttered
the zombie. "When does the
show start?"

Chapter 6
The Mystery Guest

"Well done, Lee!" beamed Mr and Mrs Price when Lee had changed back into his normal vampire clothes. "You were great!"

"Yeah," said Ollie. "That was a scream."

"Thanks," smiled Lee.

"Just one thing, Lee," said Dad. "Why did you keep

hiding during Snow Fright's
songs?"

"Yes dear," said Mum.
"Didn't you like Bella's
singing? We thought she sang
beautifully."

Lee grinned.

"Thanks Mum! I mean, er ... it's a bit of a long story. I'll explain on the way home."

Billy came over with his mum and dad.

"Phew!" said Billy. "I'm glad that's finished. Give me sums any day!"

"But you did really well,"
said Mr Price. "We loved that
bit where you knocked off the
Wicked Queen's hat. Brilliant
comic timing!"

"It wathn't meant to be funny!" came a familiar voice. "Billy totally thpoilt my hair." Accompanied by her mother, Lucy West stomped past them with her nose in the air and a furious look on her face.

"Please don't fret, Lucy poppet," said her mum. "Why doesn't Mummy buy you a present to cheer you up?"

"Too right you will!" snorted Lucy. "I want a new houthe for all my Tranthylvanian Families!"

"Yes, poppet."

"And a complete thet of My Little Zombies!" said Lucy.

"Yes, poppet."

"The really big ones, not the thtupid little ones!"

"Of course, poppet," said her mum meekly. "Anything you say."

"Good gracious, it's not just her hair that's spoilt!" said Mrs Pratt, as Lucy marched her mother out of the hall. They all laughed, though they had to agree that Lucy had actually been really good as the Wicked Queen.

But the best praise of all was
for Bella. As soon as they saw
her, Lee and the others gave
her a great cheer.

"Darling, that was amazing,"

gushed Bella's mum, giving her a hug. "Especially as you weren't feeling too well this morning."

"Yes," said her dad. "Your singing was fab."

"Er, well—" croaked Bella, but just then Miss Gargoyle came over with a very tall vampire wearing a smart suit and an elegant velvet cape.

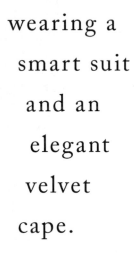

"This is our special mystery guest," said Miss Gargoyle. "Mr Harker Winegum, the owner of the Horrordrome."

"What?" blurted out Lee. "The big vampire theatre in town?"

"The very same," smiled Mr Winegum. "Now, where is Bella Williams?"

"Here," said Bella huskily.

"Delighted to meet you, Bella," said Mr Winegum, with a gracious bow. "This summer I am putting on The

Sound of Screaming. There are seven vampire children in it. After hearing you tonight, I would like to offer you a part in the show — if your parents agree?"

"Oh, Bella!" squealed her mum in delight.

"Fangtastic!" said her dad.

But Bella wasn't smiling.

"That's really nice, Mr Winegum," she

croaked. "But – but it wasn't
me singing tonight."

"Don't be silly, Bella," said
Mrs Price. "We all heard you.
You were wonderful."

Bella shook her head glumly.
"No. It wasn't me. I lost my
voice in the rehearsal. I could
just about manage to speak,

but I couldn't sing a note. My
songs were sung by – Lee!"

All eyes turned to Lee.
There were gasps of
astonishment.

"It's true," admitted Miss
Gargoyle. "Every time Snow
Fright came to a song, Lee

nipped out of sight and sang it for her."

"So that's why Gnashful kept disappearing!" said Ollie.

"Yes," said Lee. "I had the words on a piece of paper. We just had to make sure Bella was always in front of a tree

or a door or something else for me to hide behind."

"All I did was mime along," said Bella.

"It was Lee's brainwave," said Miss Gargoyle. "When Bella lost her voice it was the only way the show could go on!"

Mr Winegum stood quietly for a moment.

"Of course this means I shall have to change my offer," he said.

Bella nodded sadly.

"Lee deserves it, not me," she said.

"Never mind, darling," her mother comforted her.

Mr Winegum laughed kindly.

"No, no! You misunderstand me," he said. "I would like to offer a part in The Sound of Screaming to Lee and Bella."

"What?" cried Bella. "Really?"

"The boys and girls in the show have to act as well as sing," said Mr Winegum. "I haven't heard you sing yet, Bella,

but I do know you can act.
What do you say?"

"Yippee!" cried Bella.

"Hooray!" cried Lee.

"Excellent!" smiled Mr
Winegum. "We'll sort out
the details tomorrow. Good
evening!"

And with an
elegant swish
of his velvet
cloak, Harker
Winegum
turned – POP! –
into a bat and fluttered off.

"I can't believe we're going to be in a big show!" rasped Bella.

"Yeah, that's so cool!" said Lee.

"Hey," said Billy. "Can you get free tickets for friends?"

"Including werewolves?" said Ollie.

"You bet," said Lee. "And I'll get loads of money to buy ice cream and games and ... and ..."

"And you'll put most of it in a bank until you're older," said

Mrs Price wisely.

"And you'll still have to go to school, you know," said Mr Price.

"Aw," said Lee. "That doesn't sound like much fun."

"Oh, don't worry," grinned his mum. "You'll have a wail of a time."

"Talking of ice creams, let's celebrate!" said Mr Price.

"Scary Mary's I Scream Parlour is only around the corner."

"Yes please!" cried Lee, Bella, Billy and Ollie.

"Did someone say ice cream?" grinned Big Herb, who was just passing with a chubby grown-up vampire that looked just like Herb only older.

"OK, Herbert," said Mr Price. "You and your dad can come too."

"Yikes," whispered Lee to Ollie. "They'll run out of ice cream!"

When they reached Scary Mary's, Lee paused at the door.

"Hey," he said. "What do get
if you cross a vampire with an
ice cream?"

Everyone shook their heads.

"Frostbite!"

And to the sound of groans
and laughter, the doors of
Scary Mary's closed behind
them.

The End

Hungry for more?

Get your teeth into the next Vampire School adventure

Vampire School
Teacher Screecher

The gang are back in this fourth installment of *Vampire School*, and there's a nasty case of bat flu going about. With Miss Gargoyle

off sick, the supply teacher, Miss Fitt, quite literally turns out to be a monster - complete with neck bolts and lightning storms! Caretaker Mr Gore is up to something, but will Lee, Bella and Billy manage to find out what?

Humorous chapter books, perfect for children beginning to read on their own, these young vampires' adventures will appeal to girls and boys alike.

Vampire School
Casketball Capers

Lee, Billy and Bella are all on the St.
Orlok's casketball team.

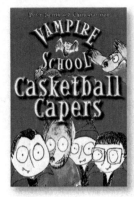

(That's the vampire
version of basketball, in
case you've never played
it.) They're all getting
ready for a big game
against the Chaney
Street werewolves. But
when the other team
arrives, it seems that some of them
aren't planning on playing a fair
game. Lee needs to come up with a
plan – fast! Will he manage to foil
the cheats before the final whistle?

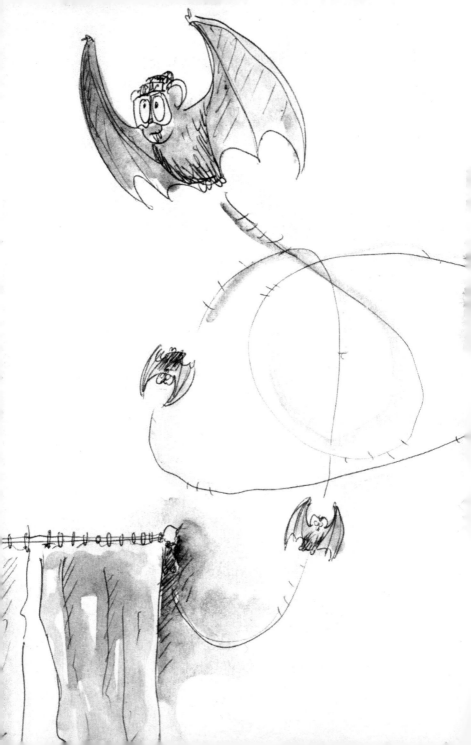

Vampire School
Ghoul Trip

Lee, Billy and Bella and the rest of Miss Gargoyle's class are off on

a school trip to the funfair. But when they arrive, there are some very strange characters hanging around. Could they have anything to do with the spate of robberies that have been happening around town? Lee, Billy and Bella decide to do some investigation and get to the bottom of the mystery.